3
5
Annie

EGMONT

We bring stories to life

First published in Great Britain in 2016
by Egmont UK Limited
The Yellow Building, 1 Nicholas Road, London W11 4AN

ISBN 978 1 4052 8147 8
62426/1
Printed in Italy

Written by Emily Stead. Designed by Claire Yeo.
Series designed by Martin Aggett.

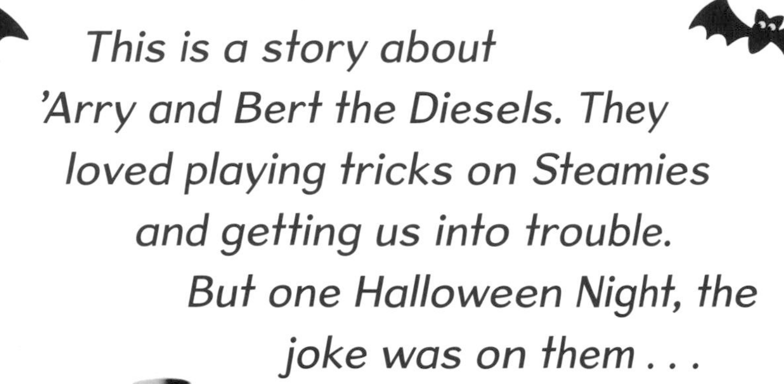

This is a story about 'Arry and Bert the Diesels. They loved playing tricks on Steamies and getting us into trouble. But one Halloween Night, the joke was on them . . .

It was Halloween on Sodor. Lots of passengers were dressed up in funny costumes!

Thomas and Emily were going on a night run. They had to collect trucks from the Smelter's Yard and deliver them to the Harbour before sunrise.

Percy was glad he hadn't been chosen for the job – working at Halloween was much too scary!

6

When Percy arrived home that evening, Thomas and Emily were just setting off on their night run.

“Be careful at the Smelter’s Yard,” puffed Percy. “It’s creepy there after dark.”

Thomas smiled. “There’s nothing to be afraid of.”

“There’s no such thing as ghosts,” Emily added, as they steamed away.

1

Thomas and Emily raced across the Island, by the light of the moon.

"**Peep! Peep!** It's very quiet tonight," said Thomas.

"And very dark," whispered Emily.

As they reached the Smelter's Yard, Emily's wheels began to **wobble** with worry.

Diesels 'Arry and Bert were nowhere to be seen, so Thomas and Emily went to look in the Shed.

"There's no need to worry," Thomas said kindly.

But suddenly there was a huge **CRASH!**

1

“**Rattling rods!** What was that?” cried Emily.

“It must have been the wind,” Thomas replied. But Thomas felt worried too.

Hiding in their Shed, ’Arry and Bert smiled. Then Bert bashed into an oil drum, sending it crashing onto the tracks. **SMASH!**

Thomas and Emily nearly jumped off the rails!

Next, the two Diesels began to wail like scary ghosts. **"Woooo!"**

"Cinders and ashes!" Thomas gasped. "This place is haunted."

Emily steamed ahead. She wanted to fetch the trucks and get out of the Yard as quickly as possible.

Emily spotted the trucks inside an empty shed. But a white sheet hanging from the ceiling caught on Emily's funnel and covered her!

"**Fizzling fireboxes!**" cried Emily. "A **ghost** has got me!"

All Thomas saw was a ghost engine coming towards him! He forgot about the trucks and whooshed away, with Emily the ghost chasing behind!

Outside, 'Arry and Bert were waiting to tease Thomas and Emily for being scaredy engines. But when they saw Thomas being chased by the ghost engine, they were scared too!

“**Help!**” cried 'Arry. “There really **is** a ghost!”

'Arry and Bert rolled away as fast as their wheels would carry them.

Thomas and the Diesels raced to Tidmouth Sheds, followed by the ghost engine.

Thomas blew his whistle loudly as a warning. **"PEEP! PEEP! Help!** There's a ghost engine after us!" he cried.

The engines all gasped when they saw it coming.

Just then, the corner of the sheet caught on a signal and Emily steamed out from underneath.

“That’s not a **ghost** – it’s just Emily!” Percy peeped.

Thomas, ’Arry and Bert felt very silly. Emily was glad there was no ghost after all, too.

The Fat Controller was cross when he heard about all the trouble that the Diesels had caused.

"You two will take the trucks to the Harbour," he told 'Arry and Bert.

He turned to Thomas and Emily. "Now we know there are **no ghosts**, we can all go back to sleep!"

The little engines had never been happier to roll into the Shed.

More about the Diesels

'Arry and Bert's challenge

Look back through the pages of this book and see if you can spot:

4
7
6
1